What Kids Say About Carole Marsh Mysteries . . .

I love the real locations! Reading the book always makes me want to go and visit them all on our next family vacation. My Mom says maybe, but I can't wait!

One day, I want to be a real kid in one of Ms. Marsh's mystery books. I think it would be fun, and I think I am a real character anyway. I filled out the application and sent it in and am keeping my fingers crossed!

History was not my favorite subject till I starting reading Carole Marsh Mysteries. Ms. Marsh really brings history to life. Also, she leaves room for the scary and fun.

I think Christina is so smart and brave. She is lucky to be in the mystery books because she gets to go to a lot of places. I always wonder just how much of the book is true and what is made up. Trying to figure that out is fun!

Grant is cool and funny! He makes me laugh a lot!!

I like that there are boys and girls in the story of different ages. Some mysteries I outgrow, but I can always find a favorite character to identify with in these books.

They are scary, but not too scary. They are funny. I learn a lot. There is always food which makes me hungry. I feel like I am there.

What Parents and Teachers Say About Carole Marsh Mysteries . . .

I think kids love these books because they have such a wealth of detail. I know I learn a lot reading them! It's an engaging way to look at the history of any place or event. I always say I'm only going to read one chapter to the kids, but that never happens—it's always two or three, at least!
—Librarian

Reading the mystery and going on the field trip—Scavenger Hunt in hand—was the most fun our class ever had! It really brought the place and its history to life. They loved the real kids characters and all the humor. I loved seeing them learn that reading is an experience to enjoy!
—4th grade teacher

Carole Marsh is really on to something with these unique mysteries. They are so clever; kids want to read them all. The Teacher's Guides are chock full of activities, recipes, and additional fascinating information. My kids thought I was an expert on the subject—and with this tool, I felt like it!
—3rd grade teacher

My students loved writing their own Real Kids/Real Places mystery book! Ms. Marsh's reproducible guidelines are a real jewel. They learned about copyright and more & ended up with their own book they were so proud of!
—Reading/Writing Teacher

"The kids seem very realistic—my children seemed to relate to the characters. Also, it is educational by expanding their knowledge about the famous places in the books."

"They are what children like: mysteries and adventures with children they can relate to."

"Encourages reading for pleasure."

"This series is great. It can be used for reluctant readers, and as a history supplement."

THE SECRET OF EYESOCKET ISLAND

by Carole Marsh

#4

Published by Gallopade International/Carole Marsh Books. Printed in the United States of America.

Managing Editor: Sherry Moss
Cover Design: Rightsyde Graphics, Inc.
Illustrations: Brittany Donaldson, Savannah College of Art & Design
Content Design: Cecil Anderson

Gallopade International is introducing SAT words that kids need to know in each new book that we publish. The SAT words are bold in the story. Look for this special logo beside each word in the glossary. Happy Learning!

Gallopade is proud to be a member and supporter of these educational organizations and associations:

American Booksellers Association
American Library Association
International Reading Association
National Association for Gifted Children
The National School Supply and Equipment Association
The National Council for the Social Studies
Museum Store Association
Association of Partners for Public Lands
Association of Booksellers for Children
Association for the Study of African American Life and History
National Alliance of Black School Educators

This book is a complete work of fiction. All events are fictionalized, and although the names of real people are used, their characterization in this book is fiction. All attractions, product names, or other works mentioned in this book are trademarks of their respective owners and the names and images used in this book are strictly for editorial purposes; no commercial claims to their use is claimed by the author or publisher.

a Word from the author

Dear Reader,

My granddaughter, Christina, and I like to speculate on "What if?" As you may know, I write mysteries set in real places that feature real kids as characters. The story is made up (fiction), but the fascinating historic facts are true (non-fiction). We are both often amused when readers guess "backwards" about what I made up and what is true in the books. Sometimes, I have a hard time being sure myself. Why? Because history is just as interesting and incredible as anything an author can make up.

So, one day, Christina and I were wondering: "What if a brother and sister lived with their fisherman father in an isolated village near the coast of Georgia? What if their father sent them on an adventure to find a mysterious island—all by themselves?" It was easy to imagine a story that could be interesting, funny, scary, and feel real. But the truth is, there are so many waterways, wetlands, and coastal islands in the area that you have a big head start on a great story, no matter what you write about!

As I told Christina about the marshes and waterways...the independent and often quirky folks who live there...the snakes, alligators, and mosquitoes who lurk there...the real-life mystery of a missing military plane—well, it all seemed Pretty Darn Scary. I hope you and Christina think so, too!

Carole Marsh

Pretty Darn Scary Books in This Series

the Ghosts of Pickpocket Plantation

the Secret of Skullcracker Swamp

the Mystery at fort thunderbolt

the Secret of Eyesocket island

table of Contents

PROLOGUE

On a little-known historic island somewhere off the Georgia/South Carolina/Florida coast wild horses roam. They are small, muscular, many shades of brown from cocoa to tree bark to teddy bear. Their hooves stamp in the sand as they look out to sea. Their manes flow like water as they run free across the hilly island.

Where did these wild ponies come from? From far across the sea long, long ago. Coming to the New World, the ships they rode on crashed to smithereens upon the sandy shoals surrounding such islands. Perhaps their masters drowned, or if lucky, were saved. The ship hulks still lie beneath the waters of the great Atlantic Ocean. And the ponies still run free.

How do they live? They thrive on the many edible grasses growing on the island. They drink from the freshwater streams and ponds. They exercise by scampering down the beaches or chasing one another over the many hammocks of sand and sea oats. They sleep beneath the stars and moon, hunkered down behind a warm sand dune.

Are they lonesome on this **desolate** island? Do they think of the past? Do they wish they had names? Do they wish they had masters? What if you roamed free—how would you feel? What would you think?

CHAPTER ONE

A STRANGE FATHER

Daniel Brickhill was a strange father. His wife had died giving birth to a boy and girl, twins. Therefore, he had been destined, as a man of honor and duty, to raise these children, though he knew nothing about children or child-rearing. The children, Simon and Frederica, did not care about these things; they loved their strange father dearly.

Daniel Brickhill was a fisherman; he had been so all his life. He could, and would (indeed, must) fish anytime and anyplace to make a living to support his family.

The Brickhill family lived in a typical ramshackle cabin in a small fishing village near the south end of the Altamaha Sound. This was his children's home, but this was not his home. His home was the sea, or the **sounds,** or the tidewater creeks—wherever fish schooled, or shrimp ran, orcrabs congregated.

Dan Brickhill's former home had been on the outskirts of London, England, where he awoke each day to the deep-throated *bonging* of Big Ben. He and his own strange father, also a widower, had lived in a similar fishing village. After just a few years of school, young Dan had joined his father on the docks and set to sea to fish the fish; it was the only life he knew.

However, Dan Brickhill knew that his children would not fish for a living. He knew this because he had promised their mother this as she had asked him, gasping, on her deathbed. And Dan Brickhill never broke a promise, most especially not to his beautiful, dying young wife.

And so, his children attended the local Buttermilk Sound School each day, faithfully, and did their homework faithfully by lantern light each night. They were bright students, eager to learn about the world beyond. That their father was illiterate was irrelevant to them—he was still the smartest man that they knew, or, so they believed, that they ever would know.

When they offered to teach their father to read and write, he scoffed, "No need! Them fish don't read, so no need me learnin' how to scrawl a note and stick it on a hook. You kids just learn for you and me both, and your mother, of course."

Because Dan Brickhill fished from dawn till dusk, and often slept overnight on trawlers at sea when the fishing was good, Simon and Frederica spent much of their time in the cabin alone. This was not a problem since they both knew how to cook, wash their clothes, clean the cabin, and study hard. But it was lonesome.

Their father feared this simple existence lacked some essential survival skill he believed that his children needed—indeed, that everyone needed, even in spite of the more newfangled life he knew was lived on the mainland—and this disturbed him greatly.

And so, on the first day that school was out for the summer that year, he devised an educational plan of his own. And a very strange plan it was, indeed!

CHAPTER TWO

THE PLAN

"Hey, Fred, pass the syrup," Dad said. He often called his daughter, Frederica, Fred when he was in a good mood.

"Sure, Dad," Frederica said with a grin. It was a beautiful late spring Saturday morning, the kind that made you thrilled you lived on the Georgia coast. The blue sky was filled with storybook clouds. The marsh had greened-up to a limeade color. The humidity was low; Dad called it "California weather." And the salty breeze off the water smelled of fresh fish, shrimp, crab, and oysters.

"What gives, Dad?" asked Simon, grabbing the syrup next. "You have that funny twinkle in your eye you get when you've thought of something for me and Frederica to do."

"Yeah," said Frederica, "usually some big, giant household chore!"

Their father laughed. He just stared at his kids for a moment. They both looked so much like their mother. He was just a crusty, old salt with sunburned skin, grizzled gray hair and beard, and long, lanky bones. But his kids were honey-colored; their Mom was part Cherokee Indian. Their hair was the pale blond of sea oats. And their eyes were the color of this morning's sky.

"Daaaaad?" Frederica prompted. "Fess up, now." It was so nice, she thought, to have their father home with them for a rare leisurely morning breakfast. Fishermen in these parts were up before dawn to catch the tide, out all day (often overnight), and home late after either taking care of the catch, or if no fish, commiserating over that unfortunate fact with their buddies down at Marley's, the local pub.

"Yeah, Dad," added Simon, putting his fists up, "or I'll have to wrestle it out of you," he teased. Simon was on the school wrestling team and was always pretending to "box" around the kitchen, jabbing at one thing or another, or putting his sister in some elaborate neck hold just to hear her squawk.

Much to his children's surprise, their father grew serious. His bleached gray eyes stared around the cabin at the weather-beaten walls, the faded handmade quilts on the rockers, and finally the hearth and mantle where a portrait of their mother was propped beside a vase of wildflowers. He straightened his shoulders, set his mouth, and gave a little nod as though some silent conversation had passed between them, some tacit agreement made. He looked back at his children and spoke to them in a tone he had never used before. It made them feel grown up.

"It's like this," he began. "There's a big world out there beyond our little fishing hamlet. You kids are good students, and I expect you'll leave here one day and go on to college and work out there somewhere in the global world, or whatever they call foreign parts, these days."

"Oh, no, Dad!" Simon interrupted. "I'm staying here and fishing with you."

"Me, too, Dad," insisted Frederica. "I want to take care of you. We love Waterway. Simon and I will never leave."

Dan Brickhill smiled wanly and shook his head. He admired his children's loyalty and devotion, but he knew in his heart that the big, wide world would draw them one day. One day soon.

He cleared his throat. "And so," he said, as if the matter of them leaving home one day was all settled, "I think you need a little more preparation. A few more survival skills. A test, if you will."

The kids looked puzzled. "But Dad," said Frederica, "we pretty much take care of ourselves now, you know. We cook and wash clothes and keep the cabin clean and get our studies done—since you're gone so much, you know?" She **abhorred** the idea that her father might find them deficient in any way.

Simon just watched their father suspiciously. He was curious what his dad was up to, but was almost afraid to ask. "You mean like Mom might have called a vision quest?" he asked.

His father gave him a look of surprised satisfaction. "Yes, son," he said. "I think that's a good way to describe this adventure I'm sending you on."

"What adventure?" asked Frederica. She was not liking the sound of this at all.

And then their dad shocked them by explaining: "I'm going to be gone all summer...signed up with Cap'n Rogers for his Grand Banks fishing gig. Figure if I don't do it now, I might get too old. Besides, it's good money and could pay some college tuition when the time comes."

"And we'll stay here all summer by ourselves?" asked Frederica, close to tears.

"Well, we sure better not be getting us any babysitter!" said Simon.

Once more, their father grew quiet. Seagulls skittered and squawked outside the window. "I don't know where you'll be," he admitted. "That will be entirely up to you."

CHAPTER THREE

A VISION QUEST

And then their father outlined his plan:

"You see, I think you guys need to get out on your own a little more. Deal with the world. Cope with the elements. Figure things out," he began.

"Huh?" grumbled Simon. "I deal with that old Ms. Rumbly, my math teacher, every day. And I always come down to the dock and help you get the catch in when the weather's bad. And I can figure out most things for myself, Dad, really."

Frederica began to smile. "I don't think that's what Dad's talking about," she said. "Let him finish."

Their father nodded and went on. "And so, I've devised an adventure—a Vision Quest, if you will—to go on this summer. I don't know how long it will take you or how you will do it, but I'm certain you will."

"You're being too mysterious, Dad," Frederica complained. "We don't have a clue what you're talking about."

"Ah!" said their father, getting up from the table. He went to the sideboard and from a drawer pulled out a small notebook. "Clues, you say?" He handed his daughter the notebook. "They're right here!"

"Clues to what?" asked Simon. He tried to snatch the notebook from his sister, but she pulled it away and held it tightly.

"Listen up!" their Dad said curtly. "This is serious. This is a mission. I'm sending you to find something, and when you find it, you can come home."

"Find what?" Frederica insisted. This whole conversation was making her very nervous. Was their father running off? Was he trying to run them off?

"Find what, Dad?" Simon asked, clearly excited about going on an adventure.

Dan Brickhill knew that his children liked mysteries and puzzles and games. He hunkered down conspiratorially across the table. "Your mission is to find an island," he said. "Eyesocket Island."

Frederica giggled at her father's mysterious antics. "Oh, Dad," she said, "you're kidding, right?"

But both children could tell by the look in their father's eyes that he was not. In fact, he looked as dead serious as he had ever looked, even at their mother's funeral.

Simon jumped up and grabbed a nautical chart off the sideboard. He scanned the index. "Hey, Dad, there is no Eyesocket Island—see," he said, turning the chart toward his father.

Dan Brickhill did not look at the map. "Yes, there is," he said softly. From his pocket, he pulled two one-hundred dollar bills and shoved them across the table toward his astounded children. "There is an Eyesocket Island, although no, you won't find it on any map."

Simon slammed his fist on the table. "And so how do we find it?"

Their father was silent.

"That's the quest, Simon," his sister said quietly. She gave her father a grave look. "You said that when **we** find this island that we could come back home. What if we don't find it?"

Dan Brickhill rose and grabbed a duffel bag from the closet and his slicker from the coat rack. He headed toward the cabin door.

"Dad!" squealed Frederica. "When are you leaving for this summer fish gig?" She looked near tears.

Her father turned and gave her a sad smile. "Now." A fleeting glimpse of pain crossed his face as he looked at his son. With a final glance at the picture on the mantle, Dan Brickhill turned and walked out the door of his cabin. He let it slam behind him and never looked back.

CHAPTER FOUR

CLUES GALORE

Now tears did roll down Frederica's face. She shoved her breakfast away. She stared at her brother. What in the world was going on, she wondered? Why had her father done that? Why had he said that? Didn't he love them anymore? Was he coming back?

Simon sat frozen at the table, his fists clenched at his side. "How are we supposed to find an island that isn't on the charts?" He seemed to be talking to himself.

"Simon!" screamed Frederica. "What are you talking about? We can't find an island that does not exist! Besides, we're just kids! Did Dad think of that?"

Taking his sister's hand, Simon said, "Take it easy, Fred. Maybe it's because we are kids that Dad's sending us on this mission. Maybe he thinks that only kids have the vision to believe in an island that's not on a map. I believe in Dad, so I believe in the island, and I believe that we can find it."

Frederica snatched her hand away. "Well, you just go find it yourself, then, smarty pants! I'm staying here. I want to spend the summer in our cabin. I want to do the things we always do—fish, and swim, and boat, and play with our friends. Put up tomatoes. Smack mosquitoes. Lay in the hammock between the old oaks and read. Don't you, Simon?"

For a moment, Simon had a lost look on his face. "I don't know," he admitted. "Sometimes I do want to go somewhere. Don't you wonder what it's like beyond Waterway? You know the only place we've ever really been is Brunswick that time Dad had his appendix taken out."

"And St. Simons with Pauly's family to see the Fourth of July fireworks that year," Frederica added. Then she confessed, "Yes, sometimes I'd like to fly on an airplane or go to the big shopping mall in Raleigh. Or New York City. Or Paris."

Simon burst out laughing. "See, Dad's right! We might want to leave here someday—maybe for a little while...maybe forever. Other kids do," he added quietly, stating the common fact that most Waterway kids' goal was to graduate high school and get as far away from the remote fishing village that was their home as possible.

"But Mom's here," his sister reminded him. After all, they took fresh wildflowers to Grove Cemetery where she was buried each Sunday after church.

Her brother got a defiant look in his eye. "I know that," he said. Then he stared at the mantle. "But you know, Fred, Mom is dead. And Dad said it best—we gotta learn to live our lives. Mom'll just have to come along. After all, a vision quest is a Native American thing, you know."

Frederica gasped and tried to think of something hateful to say back to her brother for talking about their mother that way. But suddenly, a strange peace came over her. She knew that Simon was right; their Mom was with them wherever they went. So now she surprised her brother by asking, "So how do we find this Eyesocket Island?"

Simon smiled and patted the notebook. "I think all the clues we need are in here."

"And how do we finance this quest?" Frederica asked, excitement causing her skin to tingle.

Simon waved the hundred-dollar bills in her face.

"And when do we leave?" his sister asked, the thought making her feel queasy.

Simon looked at the mantle. He looked at the door. He looked at his sister. He picked up the notebook. "Now," he said. "Right now."

CHAPTER FIVE

THE ADVENTURE BEGINS

The two kids quickly unpacked their school backpacks, and repacked them with a few travel essentials. They stuffed the precious hundred-dollar bills in their jeans' pockets, grabbed jackets they could tie around their waists, and stood in the small kitchen and looked at each other.

"What else?" Simon asked his sister.

She knew he was trying to hurry her, perhaps even hurry them both, before they changed their minds.

"The notebook!" she said, and Simon snatched it from the table. She opened the pantry and looked around, then grabbed a box of crackers and two bottles of water they had been giving away at the grocery. Then she turned to her brother and shrugged her shoulders.

As they slammed the door behind them (no one locked their doors in Waterway), Simon spotted a flashlight on the porch shelf and attached it to his backpack.

Frederica noticed some fishhooks and band-aids on a small table and picked them up. When her brother looked dubious, she said, "Well, you never know." He nodded.

They got as far as the hammock strung between the two largest oak trees in the sandy yard. The trees were probably close to one-thousand years old; they shaded the entire yard and house from the brutal summer sun. Long, gray beards of Spanish moss hung down from the lowest limbs and tickled the backs of the children's necks as they plopped down side by side in the hammock.

"What's the first clue Dad left us?" Frederica asked, watching her brother open the notebook. "We don't even have a clue of how to get started looking for Eyesocket Island unless Dad left us a really, really good first clue." She crossed both fingers.

"Ok, here goes," said Simon, breathlessly, as he read the first clue:

Before you head out on a journey, always seek sound advice and guidance.

For a moment, both kids were silent. Leaves flickered overhead, creating gold doubloon patterns on the sand beneath them.

"So what does that mean?" asked Simon.

"Leave it to Dad to be cryptic," said Frederica.

Simon gave a shove on the sand with his sneaker. "We usually go to Dad for sound advice and guidance, don't we? But he's gone."

Frederica snapped her fingers. "Maybe he means Mom? You know how he always looks at her picture on the mantle. Maybe he means we should go to the cemetery."

"And what?" her brother asked gruffly. "Ask a dead person whether to go north, south, east, or west? Yeah, right." He gave the hammock another rough shove.

Frederica sighed. "No, of course not, Simon. I just meant maybe there's another clue there, or..."

"OR!" Simon said suddenly. "Cryptic old Dad doesn't mean *sound* advice at all."

"Huh?" said his sister.

Simon was excited. This challenge was going to be one big mind game; he could already tell. "Maybe Dad doesn't mean seek sound advice, maybe he means seek advice about the Sound, you know the Sound!" He laughed.

"Oh, yeah!" said his sister. "I see what you mean. Of course—the Sound. If we are going to look for an island, I guess we will have to get on the water, and around here, all waterways lead to the Sound." She put her foot down and stopped the hammock short, almost causing her brother to fall out on the ground. "But who knows about the Sound?"

Simon jumped out of the hammock. "Why just one person around here's an expert, of course—even Dad would say that. And that's Old Man Thrush. He's an ancient mariner if there ever was one. His people came over on the slave ships, you know. And he's fished the Sound and all around all his life."

"Till now," Frederica reminded her brother. "Now he's bedridden with cancer or something. I heard he was at death's door."

"Well, come on, Fred, and let's head to Kilkenny and try to see him," Simon said, pulling his sister out of the hammock by her arm. "If he's dead, we'll be up a creek without a paddle."

"Or on the Sound without advice," Frederica corrected him.

But she found she was speaking to herself because Simon had already scampered off down the oyster shell path to the dirt road shortcut from Waterway to Kilkenny, at the point of their island.

CHAPTER SIX

OLD MAN THRUSH

"Whaaaat? You chilluns be goin' on 'bout an island with eyes?" Old Man Thrush lay back on his sagging settee and yawned, as if he were gasping for just a little extra oxygen. He was black as a wet cypress tree in the swamp, and probably as old, perhaps even one-hundred years or more.

Simon and Frederica stood erect. Simon removed his cap; their father had taught them to respect their elders.

"It's called *Eye...soc...ket* Island," repeated Frederica slowly.

"And it's not on any map or nautical chart we can find," added Simon.

Old Man Thrush shifted onto his side. He had been dipping snuff and a trickle of dark goo oozed at the side of his mouth. A tin can he used for a spittoon sat on a nearby orange crate.

The man had come to these parts as the child of slaves. The family had been lucky in that they had stayed together, and not been sold off separately. All their lives they helped grow rice and cotton, until as an older man and free, Thaddeus Thrush had gone to fishing, and a fishing whiz he turned out to be!

It seemed, the other fishermen said (at first jealous then just awed) that he could think like a fish or hear the fish's thoughts. If he was aboard your boat, he was a lucky charm, a "talisman extraordinaire," according to one boat captain.

He knew other things as well: the names of all the moons of the months; how to use plants from the forest to cure ailments; where the alligators and sea turtles would nest. Dad said it was passed down through his ancient Gullah culture that dated back to Africa.

Old Man Thrush yawned again. "Seems to me you chilluns are being tricked by your pappy. All I know is that most islands hereabouts in the Sound have been named long ago." When Simon and Frederica slumped in dejection, he quickly added, with a twinkle in his dark eyes. "But they's a knot of islands out 'bout there..." He aimed a bony, **emaciated** finger as dark as a twig to the east. "...that been scrapin' and scrabblin' over the years to make up they's mind what they be—island or sandbar, or nothing but sea bottom."

The old man stroked the salt-colored stubble on his chin. "No ones goes out that ways much...too big a chance of groundin', sinkin'. Maybe some island with eyes be that way? You needs a boat and an oily coat," he added matter-of-factly.

The kids knew he meant rain slickers. And they knew they didn't have a boat. They also could see that Old Man Thrush was now sleeping, whether because he had dozed off or as a convenient way to say that this meeting had ended, they could not tell.

As they slipped back outside, Frederica whispered, "Thank you, sir. Thank you very much."

Once outside, the two kids went to sit on Old Man Thrush's dilapidated dock. It stunk of rotten eels. Simon spread the chart out on the rough, weathered boards.

"So he could mean around here," he said, drawing a circle on an area designated UNCHARTED SANDBARS. "Dad's often commented that boats avoid this area because it's full of sandbars that are always rearranging themselves. Even the pirates avoided this area when they could, you know."

"Well, ok," said Frederica. "If that's our so-called 'Sound Advice,' then how do we get a boat and get out there and find this island so we can come back home and spend the summer?"

Her brother laughed. He looked at a cheap wristwatch he wore on his arm. "Fred, we've been gone about, uh, about a half hour now. I think this quest just might take us a little longer, don't you?"

Frederica huffed. "I think we don't have a boat and we don't have a slicker and so we might as well go home." Of course, she knew she didn't really mean that. Finally she sighed. "Read another clue."

Simon nodded and opened the notebook. But before he could find the right page, the *chuk-chuk-chuk* of a motor brought a small boat with a small man right up to the dock.

It was clear that the man was drunk, perhaps on drugs. His khaki work clothes were disheveled and he had a fresh bruise over his left eye.

"Hi-yo, kids," he said. "You kids got any money? I'm lookin' to sell this here boat. I got to get some money to buy a bus ticket and get back home. Make ya a real deal."

Simon and Frederica exchanged astounded looks. Could Old Man Thrush's Gullah magic have arranged this? They doubted it.

"Uh," said Simon, "we might be interested. "What do you want for that piece of junk?" A piece of junk is what the boat actually was. You could see daylight through some rusted spots near the bow and the motor gave off a stinky wisp of smoke.

The man stroked his chin. "How 'bout five-hunnered?"

Simon laughed and started to get up. His sister resisted the urge to pull him back down.

"Well, three-hunnered, then," the man said grouchily.

"One hundred," said Simon. "Take it or leave it."

Without another word, the man revved the motor and pulled away from the dock.

"*Simon*," cried Frederica. "He's leaving!"

Much to their surprise, the man brought the boat about and returned to the dock. "Alright, alright," he said. It was clear he needed the money and was constantly looking over his shoulder as if someone was chasing him.

Simon just picked up the notebook and turned the page. He read the clue, then turned the page so only his sister could see it and read:

Be prepared to pay your way; no one else will.

Frederica smiled. It was half their money gone awfully quickly, but they needed the boat and the clue seemed to be Dad's way of saying they wouldn't be coming home with any money in their pockets. She nodded at her brother.

"Deal," Simon said to the man, who handed the tie line to the boy and snatched the one-hundred dollar bill from his hand. He sped off with neither a word nor a look back.

Simon tugged the boat snug to the dock so that they could board. It was only then that they saw the name of the boat in faded black on the stern:

DOOMED

CHAPTER SEVEN

UNDERWAY

"Do you think it was good for us to spend half our money so quickly?" Frederica asked her brother as he steered the boat through the narrow waterway.

Simon shrugged as he finessed the rudder gently back and forth to keep them in the channel. "I guess so," he admitted. "Otherwise, we'd still be land-bound, and that would not get us out on the water so we could search for Eyesocket."

Frederica nodded. "Yeah, I think we need to be on the water to find an island, that's for sure. Besides, hurricane season is underway; Dad knew that. I figure he thinks this will be easy for us, with all his clues. We can find the island and get back home. It's not safe for two kids to be out on their own in treacherous waters, you know."

Simon surprised her by laughing. "Look around, Fred," he said. "It's not treacherous at all. It's a perfect day to be on the water."

Frederica gazed out at the marsh, which ranged as far as she could see. She frowned at her brother. "You know what I mean. Things can change fast on the water. Look at all the close calls Dad's had." Her voice trailed off as she and her brother recalled the long nights when the fishing boat their father had been aboard had not come in, had not been seen, and no word heard from. He had always come back...so far.

Soon, in spite of the stress of embarking on such a strange adventure, the two children succumbed to the magic of the wetlands. They knew that most people who didn't live in the low country of North and South Carolina and Georgia had no clue as to the importance of what was generally referred to as wetlands.

They might eat in fancy restaurants in Raleigh or Atlanta or Columbia, but have no idea that the salt marsh was the incubator for an endless supply of shrimp, oysters, fish, crabs, and the organisms that fed them—endless, that is, unless developers overbuilt the land for homes and businesses, and shopping centers, and parking lots.

"The wetlands are the lungs of the land," their father always said. "If you want clean water and healthy seafood, you'd better protect them."

Each tidal cycle was like inhaling and exhaling, with breaths either of clean water, or pollution. It was a constant (often ugly, and always political) battle between those who wanted the coast kept pristine and those who wanted to mine or fill the marshes.

Frederica smiled. It actually felt good to be underway, she thought. No matter what might happen, at least they were trying. "Are we headed where I think we're headed?" she asked her brother.

Simon was so absorbed in admiring the views and navigating the small boat in the narrow corridor of water that Frederica had to repeat her question. But Simon interrupted her: "Look at the next clue and see what you think," he said with a grin.

His sister took the notebook and turned the page. The clue made her giggle:

Hoigh toide, low toide.
Rub-a-dub-dub, an old woman in a tug.
Make your way; see what she has to say.

"Well Dad knew we'd figure that clue out easy enough," Frederica said. Simon nodded.

At least it was not very far by water to Miz Emmeline's house, Frederica thought. The woman was a descendant of some of the early Elizabethan English who made their way to these islands hundreds of years ago. Even now, their distinctive accents set them apart. They pronounced high "hoigh" and tide "toide." "The Queen's English," Miz Emmeline called it.

The old woman lived on a tugboat at the end of Sapelo Island. It was a lonesome spot and Frederica knew it would be their true jumping off point to search for Eyesocket.

However, as she and Simon well knew, the picture-book water could turn into a life or death struggle at any turn. And for them, this turn was right around the bend.

CHAPTER EIGHT

BETWEEN A ROCK AND A HARD PLACE

Just as Frederica leaned back and propped on her brother's knobby knees, wishing they could just gunkhole and read a book or something, Simon's legs stiffened.

"Sorry," his sister said.

"It's not that," Simon whispered. "Look ahead!"

Frederica did not like the sound of fear in her brother's voice. Simon was not afraid of much of anything, so she was truly petrified to sit up straight and see what was coming toward them. For one thing, she guessed what the problem was, and unfortunately, she was right.

At first, she could just see the tell-tale triangle of black buttons breaking the surface of the water. Then immediately, the hooded black eyes and snout, wearing a coat of green algae, rose out of the water. A flick of a tail far behind indicated that the alligator stroking toward them was a whopper.

Frederica held her breath as Simon tried to put the motor in reverse. The gator paused as if waiting to see if they were prey or not worth his attention. Frederica prayed he would decide to ignore them.

Simon knew better.

CHAPTER NINE

GATOR ACRES

The area they were in was often called Gator Acres. There had always been alligators in these parts, but more so the last few years after the American alligator had been removed from the endangered species list. Since then, the alligator population from Florida to Virginia had increased so much, that an official alligator-hunting season was being considered. From the size of this gator, he had been around long before any of these discussions had taken place. The kids knew that alligators dated back to prehistoric times, but unlike many dinosaurs, all gators were meat eaters. And this one looked hungry. Or at least he looked. And looked. And looked.

The motor would not start. It was like a standoff, with the bow of their small boat almost nose to nose with the scute-covered snout of the alligator.

"He's holding his ground," Simon whispered.

"Then he must be a she," said Frederica. "A mother guarding her nest."

"Exactly the kind of gator that you should never mess with," said Simon with a nervous sigh. They both knew that the gator was either guarding a nest behind her, or, worst-case scenario, behind them. If that were the case, they were in big trouble since there was no room to turn around.

Worst of all, they realized, the boat was low, and gators could jump. Most people didn't know that an alligator could leap out of water. The two children felt doomed. They each had run from startled alligators on land. Another thing most folks didn't know was that an alligator can run fast for a short distance. When they stand up, their stubby legs are strong and they can dash right at you. Fortunately, they can't run in a zigzag pattern, and Simon and Frederica had run back and forth more than once to escape a gator, usually a small one. They had learned to look where they walk, especially where alligators might sun, or where shadows might hide the dark green creatures.

But today there was no hiding. They sat so still that they could hear the sound of the rising tide sift through the skinny blades of marsh grass. The current seemed to glide around the contours of the alligator. But then, he moved toward them.

"Simon!"

"I know," Simon said. "Just be still." He reach down and grabbed an oar. The gator flicked the tip of her tail as if to say, "Whatcha gonna do with that toothpick, boy?"

Then suddenly, they all were startled by the roar of a large, powerful motor. A fishing skiff, filled with teens, appeared behind them. The driver barely stopped the boat before it crashed into Simon and Frederica. The gator made a large splash and vanished.

Simon wasted no time. "Can you help us?" he asked the boat's driver, who just laughed at him.

"What? Help a couple of snotty nose kids? Why?" the driver said, then turned over the side of his boat and puked into the water.

A girl in the back of the boat seemed concerned. "You got a problem?" she asked gently.

Frederica spoke up. "Our motor's dead and we can't get turned around. Can you help us, please?"

When the girl looked nervous, Frederica realized that she knew there were alligators in these shallow waters. She looked hesitant, then shoved her boyfriend in the ribs. "Help them!" she insisted. "So we can get out of here. And you drive. Jason's drunk as a skunk. We should never have come out with him."

The boy nodded and grabbed a small toolbox. He jumped in the smaller boat, almost overturning it. For a few minutes he and Simon hovered over the silent motor, which suddenly choked to life.

"Wow, thanks!" said Simon.

"You need to get this junker to a shop," the boy advised.

"I know," said Simon, "but right now we just need to get out of here." The boy motioned for the girl to toss him a rope. He tied the line to the rowboat, then jumped back into the bigger boat. He shoved the boy named Jason out of the way and started the motor. Slowly he reversed backwards, tugging the small boat along.

Soon, they were in a larger part of the channel, and the boy maneuvered so that the rowboat was ahead of them. Then he nodded for Simon to loosen the line and toss it back to them.

"Thank you so much!" Frederica said. She gave them a big smile.

"Appreciate it," Simon said more soberly. He did not like to depend on other people.

"No problem," said the boy. "Get to a shop now, ok?"

"You kids be careful out here," said the girl. "You don't even have any lifejackets." She looked worried.

"We'll be ok now," Frederica promised. The two crafts were parted by the drifting tide and idling motors. The other boat turned off down another channel.

"Probably headed to get rid of that puking boy," said Simon.

"And where are we headed?" his sister asked.

Simon set his chin into the wind and spun the boat around. "Same place," he said. "That's what the clue calls for and this is the only way."

"Siiiiiimon," pleaded Frederica. "What about the gator?"

CHAPTER TEN

THE LADY BEE

This time there was no sign of an alligator, or any other form of life for that matter. The sun was at high noon and most of the water creatures had headed for shadow and shade, hunkering down in the hottest part of the day.

A slow, but uneventful trip took them right up to Miz Emmeline's tugboat. Faded letters on the side read LADY BEE. The boat was a nautical disaster.

As they approached Miz Emmeline's tugboat, the orange orb of sun was sinking into the baby blue water glistening behind the stern of the pathetic hulk. You could even see light spewing through cracks in the rotting boards. Surely the boat was sitting on the mud down below, hopefully stuck so deeply in the muck that even a storm would not disturb Miz Emmeline's home.

As Simon pulled their little boat alongside the lopsided dock to tie up, a rat's nest of gray curls appeared overhead.

"'Bout time you chirren got here," Miz Emmeline screeched down at them. "Dark's a'comin.' Dark's a'comin'," she repeated, glancing fearfully at the horizon as if a silhouette of a pirate's *joli rouge* might appear at any moment.

"Yes, ma'am," said Frederica, tugging at the line to get it secure around the mooring post. Simon hopped out to help.

After tying up, they scampered up the gangplank, which flapped left and right. They had to step over the missing "teeth" of boards that had long ago fallen into the water.

A gnarled gray hand reached out to help them each aboard the rattletrap ship that had long since been stripped of its fishing gear, trawl doors, nets and lines, leaving only an old woman and two gray cats. For all the kids knew, the boat didn't even have an engine any longer. But what it did have, surprised them.

As they followed Miz Emmeline below, they were stunned to discover that she had turned the sad stateroom into all but an English parlor! A thousand patterns of paisley and plaid, surely collected over a lifetime, covered chairs and sofas and rocking chairs and even tables.

The cozy room was aglow with light from hanging kerosene lanterns. A silver teakettle burbled on a pot-bellied stove, its door open to reveal glistening red coals. A cat stretched in each porthole and watched the elaborate proceedings as Miz Emmeline settled the children into overstuffed armchairs and prepared the tea set on the gaily-covered table.

"What are you chirren doing out here in these convoluted waters at night?" Miz Emmeline asked. "Does your daddy know what you're up to?" As she questioned them, she poured tea into flowered china cups and presented them with warm chocolate chip cookies.

Simon and Frederica grinned at one another. They were starving, and what a surprise this warm respite was. It sure made them miss home, already, and their journey had just begun. Would each day be this long, frightening, and unending, Frederica wondered to herself.

Adroitly, Simon skewed their answer to the old woman's questions. "Oh, we're just on a little summer adventure," he said. "We got a little out of the channel and spotted your boat and thought we'd drop by."

Neither child missed the suspicious shadow that crossed the old woman's face. Their father would say that Miz Emmeline was no fool. But they were relieved when she did not question them further.

"Well, you're sure off the beaten path," the woman said. "More than that, off the chart. No one comes out in these waters if they can help it," she added.

"Why not?" Frederica couldn't help but ask, even though she'd rather change the subject.

Miz Emmeline sipped her steaming tea. Her old eyes were pale gray, her face an island of wrinkles, each surely with a story to tell. As it turned out, she had plenty of stories to tell them, as she kept the tea and cookies coming.

"The islands out this way are on the fringe between land and sea," Miz Emmeline began. "Sometimes I think they don't know what they want to be—water, marsh, land, here, there, somewhere else. Erosion gnaws away as they shift and move about over time. Sand fills in a clear channel overnight, and when a blustery nor'easter comes along, it's like fruitcake turnover or musical chairs," she said with a laugh and a shake of her curls. "If you know your way through the maze one day, well, you won't the next. It's just not worth the hassle for boaters, just as the buccaneers of long ago learned."

"Pirates?" asked Frederica.

"Oh, yes!" said Miz Emmeline, not even flinching when a cat pounced on her lap and began to purr. "During the Golden Age of Piracy, these islands were some of their hideouts. At Christmas, they'd have a big feast called a Saturnalia, where they cooked meat on a rotisserie spit over an open fire."

"Like barbecue?" Simon interrupted.

"Exactly like barbecue!" the old woman agreed. "It was called *boucan*, and that's how they got their name of *boucaniers* or buccaneers."

She stroked the cat's fur and continued her tale. "Those crazy pirates chased one another all around these parts, trying not to get snared in the invisible sand clutching up from the sea bottom. Sometimes, they stopped to drydock their ships and scrape the barnacles off the bottom, which slowed them down. They were vulnerable then, and if they got caught, it was doomsday for them!"

"Good thing we don't have pirates anymore," Frederica said, peering out the porthole, now filled with stars instead of sunset.

Miz Emmeline let out a big squawk so loud that the kids wondered if she had a parrot! "No pirates today? Why, chile, nothing could be further from the truth!"

"Yeah, Fred," Simon said. "I think we ran into some today!"

Remembering, his sister nodded in agreement.

"How's that?" the old woman said, the suspicious shadow crossing her face once more. The children exchanged glances, wondering if she was just old, senile, or had some disease of the aged like dementia or Alzheimer's.

When her face cleared, Simon got brave and asked, "Do you know of an island named Eyesocket?"

To their surprise, Miz Emmeline sat straight up, as if she had been startled by a ghost. The cat fled from her lap. "What? What?" she demanded, looking around the room in fear. "What makes you ask of Eyesocket? How would you know that name? Why do you seek such an island?"

The children were confused and a little afraid.

"Dad told us about it," Frederica said quickly, hoping that would calm the old woman down and it did, somewhat.

She sighed and sat back in her chair. "You don't want to go there," she assured them. It sounded more like a defiant warning. "You get to Eyesocket, you might not get back."

That *definitely* sounded like a warning.

CHAPTER ELEVEN

JOLI ROUGE

Miz Emmeline insisted that the children spend the night aboard. While they were relieved, they wondered what she thought they were going to do—strike out in the dark for home? The thought made Frederica shiver.

"Those sure were good chocolate chip cookies," Simon **complimented** the woman, as she steered them toward two small bunkrooms below down a narrow passageway.

"Do you know why they're called chocolate?" she asked, with a twinkle in her eye.

Frederica laughed. "Because they're made with chocolate chips."

Miz Emmeline shook her gray mass of hair. "No! This recipe was named after the plantation I once lived on. It was called Chocolate."

Frederica was fascinated. "A plantation called Chocolate?" It sounded like something out of a fairy tale.

The old woman got a dreamy, faraway look in her eyes. "Yes," she said softly. "My Chocolate Plantation. But that was a long time ago."

Simon asked. "Is it near Eyesocket Island?"

The woman was instantly stern. "To bed—now! I don't know what your daddy is thinking, two kids out in the dark in a leaky, old boat." As she continued to mutter to herself, she turned and headed back for the main cabin, leaving the children to make their own way to their creepy quarters below.

"I hope there aren't rats," Frederica whispered.

"I hope this thing doesn't sink in the night," Simon responded.

Soon, they had tucked themselves into the narrow, rock-hard bunks and tugged dank-smelling covers up to their chins. That night, Frederica dreamed of teacups and chocolate, of plantations and pirates, and of eyes and eyesockets...empty, frightening eyesockets. She also felt sure that she heard a man's voice and things being brought aboard the *Lady Bee*.

The next morning, sunshine poured in through their porthole windows. When Frederica woke up, stretched and threw back her blanket, Simon was already dressed and sitting cross-legged on his bunk, Dad's book open to the next page.

"What sayeth the book?" Frederica asked with a giggle.

"Don't be-eth silly," Simon said, and tossed a pillow at her. "We *are* near this stupid Eyesocket Island," he said seriously. "I can feel it. I can smell it."

"All I smell is damp, moldy wood, and maybe mouse droppings," Frederica said.

"The head's ok," Simon said, nodding to a small door. Frederica grabbed her clothes and scampered to the tiny bathroom.

When she returned to their bunkroom, she could smell bacon cooking in the small galley overhead. Simon read aloud:

Follow the whales and follow the horse
Go by air to stay on course.

"Wow," said Frederica. "Dad must be crazy to think we can figure out all these obtuse clues. There are no whales. And does he mean...a seahorse? And, sure, Dad, we'll just grab a flight at Savannah-Hilton Head International Airport. I'm sure our $200 will get us tickets to, to, to...where?"

"$100," Simon corrected his sister. "We're down to one-hundred bucks."

"Breakfast!" Miz Emmeline hollered and they heard cats bound across the cabin floor.

"Let's eat and be on our way," Simon said. "Time's a-wasting. You know, Dad never said it would take us all summer to find Eyesocket. So, let's get the job done so we can go home."

"I'm all for that," Frederica said, slipping her shoes on and dashing off to breakfast.

"Tell us more about Chocolate Plantation," Frederica begged, as Miz Emmeline served them bacon, eggs, grits, and scones, which she told them were English biscuits.

Simon gave his sister a look. He was ready to leave.

But the lonesome old woman, clearly refreshed after a night's sleep, was eager to recount the tale of her past:

"The natives were here first, of course, and the Spanish came to the New World, but it was we English who stuck. We came, some poor, some prisoners, but all of us looking for a better life. Ships full of men, women, chirren, animals. Ships wrecked on shoals, sandbars; it wasn't a pretty picture. Some of us never got very far inland. My ancestors sure didn't. My people have lived in these parts almost 400 years."

"And what about the pirates?" Frederica egged her on, in spite of another "look" from her brother.

Frederica could have sworn that Miz Emmeline's gray cheeks blushed. "Oh, you no-never-mind what I said last night." It sounded like a pleading tone in her voice. "The pirates came later, and went. Any pirates today are just passing-through meanies, or irate, ill-in-the head old-timers."

Simon couldn't help himself. "And Eyesocket Island?"

Now Miz Emmeline ducked her head. When she looked back up, her eyes were steady. "Forget that island," she said, kindly, no sound of warning now. "Head on back home and tell your daddy I said hello. Go enjoy your summer. You're only chirren such a short time."

Simon looked at his sister. He felt sure that the old woman was hornswaggling them with sweet talk. He realized that she was not only old, but shrewd and persuasive. He also felt that they were being dismissed. That was fine with him.

But when they said their good-byes and headed down the rickety gangplank, they stopped cold: The DOOMED was gone!

CHAPTER TWELVE

DOOMED AGAIN

"Somebody stole our boat!" Simon cried.

Miz Emmeline looked put out. "Who'd steal that sieve," she said. Then she laughed. "Look closer, boy!"

Frederica saw what the old woman meant, but it wasn't funny. "Look, Simon," she said. "Our boat sunk!"

Sure enough, the outline of the DOOMED could be seen just a few inches beneath the water. It was a goner.

Everyone was silent. Miz Emmeline seemed agitated, as if she were more inconvenienced than the children. Suddenly, she snapped her bony fingers together in a loud pop. "I got it!" she said. "There's an old dinghy rat-holed beneath the stern deck. Tied up tight under there." From somewhere beneath her swaddled clothes, she pulled a fishing knife. "Cut her loose!" she ordered, handing Simon the weapon—blade first. Dad would have croaked, he thought.

Gingerly, Simon retrieved the knife. Making his way cautiously out onto the platform at the back of the boat, he saw that a small dinghy was tied beneath.

As he cut one line loose, then another, the small craft plopped into the water and floated toward them.

Frederica groaned. "Oh, Simon, it looks worse that the other boat."

"It does," her brother agreed, "but it's floating."

The boat floated nearer and Simon grabbed the line and tugged her closer. In faded letters on the starboard side of the boat were the letters:
STINGER.

"What kind of name is that?" Frederica asked.

"Who cares?" said Simon. He noticed Miz Emmeline was strangely silent. She seemed to be eager for them to leave. He decided to test that. "I guess we'd better shove off before this one sinks, too," he said.

The old woman nodded eagerly. "Here!" she said, producing a package. "Take this. Be careful."

Biting her lip, Frederica lowered herself down into the pathetic, little dinghy. Simon followed quickly and the weight of his body caused the boat to sink nearly to its gunnels. Before he had time to check to see if any safety gear, or anything else for that matter, was aboard, the craft quickly drifted with the current. "Grab an oar!" he told his sister, who was busy waving goodbye to Miz Emmeline.

As Simon poled the boat away from the bank and the tugboat, his sister scrambled around looking for something to paddle with. Just as they were almost out of earshot, he heard Miz Emmeline holler something across the water to them. He looked up and shrugged his shoulders indicating that he could not hear her. She cried out again. Once more, Simon shook his head.

Red-faced, Frederica surfaced from the bottom of the boat empty-handed. "What did she say?" she asked her brother.

Simon turned away. He did not want to admit that he thought he'd heard the old woman say something about Eyesocket Island. But what—well, they would never know.

CHAPTER THIRTEEN

TO THE END OF THE EARTH

Simon had a pretty good idea that they were closer to Eyesocket Island than Miz Emmeline had let on. He let his sister pole to keep the boat in the narrow channel while he hooked up a ratty gas motor. He also found a short mast and a tattered sail in the bow of the boat, but left them there. Once the motor sputtered to life, he took over the rudder. "Yeah," complained Frederica. "I get gator watch again."

"No," Simon assured her. "The tide's running fast. I just want you to keep an eye out for any side channels. They come up fast in this tall marsh grass. Call out as quick as you spy one to port. I want us to head east all we can."

Frederica nodded. The last thing they needed to do was wander around in circles in this endless maze of wetlands. She felt sure that there would be no old woman in a tugboat in their path today. They would be on their own, and she would just as soon be camped on some island—any island—versus sleeping in this leaky teacup of a boat.

She and her brother had little to say as they journeyed through the beautiful wetlands. The iridescent water and lush greens belied the fact that there were gators, snakes, toe-snapping crab claws, mosquitoes, gnats, spiders, and plenty of other creepy-crawlies lurking in most every wet nook and cranny.

Frederica spied a number of channels—some larger, some smaller—to the port side of the boat and Simon maneuvered them into each one. At each channel that appeared to starboard, Frederica craned her neck to see what might lie in that direction.

Simon read her mind. "You know what Yogi Berra said?" he asked her.

"No," said Frederica. She wondered if he meant Yogi Bear.

But Simon said, "He's a famous baseball player who said, 'When you come to a fork in the road—take it!'"

"Huh?" said his sister. "And what does a baseball player know about the sea?"

"I think you missed the point," Simon groused. They were getting tired. He shoved the boat into some reeds and they stopped and snacked on the chocolate chip cookies Miz Emmeline had given them.

"Where do you think Chocolate Plantation is?" Frederica asked.

"Is or was," Simon said. "Most plantations hereabouts are gone, or ruins. I doubt there's anything to see of those good old days."

"They weren't good old days," Frederica corrected. "It took slave labor to run those plantations."

"I know," said Simon. "Dad says life on a plantation was hard for everyone. He said it was pretty much a life of unrelenting misery: mud, flood, disease, sickness, all the work done by hand—it was no fun."

Frederica trickled her fingers through the cool water. "Maybe, but it sure sounds nice, doesn't it? Chocolate Plantation."

Simon giggled. "You'd have to wear a big, fancy dress with petticoats and stuff."

His sister bristled. "Not me! I guess I'd..." She stopped talking mid-sentence.

"What is it?" Simon asked. He grabbed the knife that he realized he'd accidentally kept. His sister had clearly seen something, but what, he wondered.

"Shhhh," Frederica whispered. "I think I just saw...a pirate!"

CHAPTER FOURTEEN

AVAST!

They hove-to as long as they could. But they neither saw nor heard anything else, certainly no sign of a buccaneer.

"I really did see something," Frederica promised her brother. "I just got a fleeting glimpse. A black hat, an eye patch—just a glimpse of a head above the cord grass as some boat drifted by just over there."

"I said I believe you," Simon said yet again. "But it's gonna get dark. I think we ought to move on."

Frederica nodded, but when Simon tried the motor, it would not start.

"What now?" Frederica cried. "We can't stay here all night, Simon; we just can't."

"Keep you knickers on," Simon said. "We've got daylight enough." He climbed into the bow and hauled out the mast and sail. Quickly, he set the mast and tied the sail in place.

"Oh, yeah, that swiss cheese handkerchief will get us someplace fast," said Frederica. "Why right to the Holiday Inn in Brunswick in no time, I'll bet." She folded her arms over her chest and pouted.

"Got a better idea?" her brother barked back, when suddenly, they were both almost jerked overboard as the freshening breeze caught the sail and pushed them forward in the channel.

"Wow!" said Frederica. "We're underway."

"But underway to where?" said Simon.

"I don't know," his sister admitted, "but I think we're gonna get there fast!"

In fact, the breeze quickly climbed the Beaufort Scale as it grew stronger each hour. By dusk, they were almost afraid that they would be sucked out to sea. They scooted effortlessly through the water. The little boat seemed to have a mind of its on, even taking the port channels.

Soon, the sky turned lavender and stars twinkled overhead. The two children went from the joy of finally moving to fear of spending the night in strange waters with no shelter and no food, perhaps with pirates on the prowl.

But suddenly, they had no choice: the boat slammed into a mud bank and stopped. The mast toppled, shredding the sail into pieces as it fell.

The thud sent the children reeling. Both grabbed to stay aboard, then latched on to one another.

"We're ok," Frederica finally whispered.

"Yeah," said Simon.

And then it started to thunder, then rain, then lightning streaked great zigzags across the sky.

CHAPTER FIFTEEN

THE WORST NIGHT OF THEIR LIVES

It was the worst night of their lives. The two children huddled in the bottom of the boat, clinging to one another and whatever else they could find. Simon had grabbed the pieces of sail to wrap around them, but they still felt like wet mummies! The chocolate chip cookies had long since washed away.

And yet, somehow, just before dawn, they slept. And as they slept, the sun came out. This was good, because when they woke up, they both could clearly see that they had crashed upon a small island upon which stood, not a plantation, but a very swanky modern house.

But that was in the distance. In the foreground, what the two, wet, filthy children saw was a pair of tall black boots, then a large hand, which reached down to pull them to their feet.

"Kids," a deep voice boomed. "This is a private island. You're trespassing!"

Simon and Frederica tried to explain, but the man would not listen. He grabbed both of them up under his arms, and carted them down a long boardwalk and up the wide steps of a low country-style house to the veranda.

With one of his booted feet, he kicked at the double front doors, filled with seabirds in etched glass surrounded by glistening brass trim. Over the door was a large, weathered board with the word OATFIELDS engraved in fanciful letters.

Quickly, the sound of feet padded across the hardwood floors and a large black woman opened the door.

"Laws, sake, Mr. Nebble, what you got there?!" The woman opened the double doors wide, allowing the man to enter the house and deposit the two children upon a beautiful Oriental carpet.

Simon and Frederica looked up at the enormous crystal chandelier hanging over their heads...at the man dressed in a stylish business suit with a navy blue tie that matched his eyes...and the black woman in a white apron with her hands pressed firmly on her hips.

The children could not think of a single sensible thing to say. So, finally, Simon squeaked, "Do you sell boats?"

The man rared back and roared with laughter. Wrinkles flared beside his eyes. "No," he said, "I sell stocks and bonds." He thrust a thumb back toward the waterway. "But I can certainly see why you might be in the market for a boat, son. What I can't understand is how you got way out here in that highly unsuitable craft."

"Laws, Mr. Nebble, that don't matter!" said the housekeeper. "These children are wet, cold, and, excuse me, please—plum nasty. Let me get them cleaned up before you give them the third degree."

Mr. Nebble nodded and stepped back. "Of course, Mathilda. I shall receive these two ragamuffins in the sunroom in ten minutes," he said, then spun on the shiny black dress shoes that had been hidden beneath his gum boots and strode into his nearby office. The kids could easily see that it contained computers and printers and a large screen plasma monitor showing the stock market ticker from the Stock Exchange on Wall Street in New York City. They were impressed and astounded.

Without another word, the housekeeper clutched both kids by their wrists and tugged them into a large laundry room with a half-bath where she told them to wash up. She thrust thick, white terrycloth robes at them and headed to the kitchen.

As they took turns scrubbing at the large sink, they could overhear Mathilda muttering to herself in the kitchen as she put on a teakettle.

"Crazy children. What they doing out here in the nautical boondocks. Mr. Nebble won't be happy. He likes his privacy. We never have visitors out here unless he flies them in. Laws, laws, what's next?"

As the kids eavesdropped while they cleaned up, Simon pointed out the window. Frederica nodded at the yacht-size sailboat docked nearby. Then she pointed and Simon nodded back. He, too, spotted the small Gulfstream airplane positioned on a paved runway.

While Mathilda continued to mutter to herself and clang china teacups, and the water from the teakettle began to steam and hiss, the two children knew what they had to do.

Simon nodded at his sister and she nodded back. They had already put on the robes, so that was too bad, but there was no time. As quickly as they could, they slipped out the side door and made a run for it!

CHAPTER SIXTEEN

RUN FOR YOUR LIVES

Like blue herons slipping away from a predator, Simon and Frederica dashed toward the aircraft. They boarded through the hatch-like door on the far side. It was a fancy four-seater. The kids climbed as far back into the fuselage as possible and tugged a tarp up over their heads.

From their hiding place, they could hear the ruckus on the porch.

"Laws, laws, Mr. Nebble, they was right here...right here in the laundry. I made them chocolate. They looked so scrawny and cold, you know? I'm sorry. Where could they go?" Mathilda was clearly in a panic.

But Mr. Nebble was as calm as could be. "It's very curious, Mathilda," he said. On the porch, he scanned the horizon, slowly and steadily. He looked one way, then the other, then repeated his search. "Very strange," he went on. "Those two kids should not be out this far. It's dangerous. Riptides. Sharks. Alligators. Pirates."

When Frederica gave her brother a petrified look, he whispered in her ear. "Don't worry. He's just kidding. I think he's guessing we can hear him. He just wants to scare us."

"Well, he's doing a darn good job!" said Frederica.

"Shhh!" hissed Simon.

Now they heard footsteps pounding their way across the dock. "Don't worry about it, Mathilda," Mr. Nebble called back over his shoulder. "I imagine those two hooligans are long gone by now. Trespassing is a serious crime. So is child endangerment. I'd just like to know what kind of parents they have to allow youngsters to gallivant about in such a hazardous environment."

Frederica felt tears sting her eyes. She did not want anyone to think bad of her father.

"Shhhhhhh!" Simon reminded his sister as the footsteps grew closer. Sure enough, the man was headed to the plane.

"I've got to get to New York, Mathilda," Mr. Nebble said. "You hold down the fort, you hear. Put the cocoa and cookies on the porch," he advised. "If they vanish, well, you'll know those two varmints are still around. This is a private island. They'll learn that, soon enough."

Mathilda mumbled something back. Frederica thought she was crying. Just the thought of hot cocoa and cookies made her tummy rumble; she was starving.

It was all the two kids could do not to gasp when the door to the plane opened and Mr. Nebble climbed inside. He slammed the door behind him. They could hear the noises of straps and other "getting ready to fly" sounds.

"Who's the pilot?" Frederica mouthed silently to her brother.

That question was quickly answered by Mr. Nebble's voice. "Brunswick Tracon, this is GS 2348, taking off from Oatfields, headed out to sea to Savannah to fuel up."

As the man gave the rest of his coordinates and a voice responded in the affirmative to every comment, the plane began to taxi down the runway. Frederica was petrified; she had never been in an airplane before.

Simon, on the other hand, was excited. This was the kind of adventure he'd always wanted to have. He couldn't stand it another moment. Carefully, he slipped the tarp away just enough so that he could peek out the window.

He was not careful enough. The pilot had caught the small movement out of the corner of his eye. "There you are!" he shouted above the engine noise. "I should have known!"

Suddenly, the plane swooped up into the air. Frederica gasped aloud.

"You two hold on back there," Mr. Nebble ordered. "We're coming around."

By now, the plane was already out over the edge of the Atlantic Ocean. The kids could easily see the lush islands below with their edges of glistening white sand charged by blue waves dressed in white ruffles of sea foam.

"What's that?" Simon asked. He pointed to a string of objects in the water below.

Mr. Nebble laughed. "A treat to see!" he called back. "Atlantic Right Whales. They migrate along the coast this time of year. Let's take a look!"

Suddenly, the plane banked. Frederica felt her stomach do a U-turn. And then the aircraft sped up the coastline just over the whales, which the children thought were beautiful and delightful to watch.

"Oh, Simon," Frederica said, mesmerized by the sight that she knew few people ever saw. But then she quickly added: "OH, SIMON!"

"I know, I know," her brother said. "I see them."

"No, no!" said Frederica, pointing inland.

The airplane banked sharply without warning—but not before the two children saw the island up close and clearly. It was shaped sort of like a light bulb. Two perfectly round ponds filled with freshwater created two blue eyes. A sliver of sand made a nose. And a craggy area carved out of the marsh made a mouth. It was just like a skull...a scary skull.

"Eyesocket Island," Simon whispered.

"You kids weren't supposed to see that," Mr. Nebble muttered. The airplane banked again, then again, and before the kids could settle their topsy-turvy stomachs, the Gulfstream came in for a smooth landing right back on the runway from which it had taken off just a few minutes earlier.

CHAPTER SEVENTEEN

SIMON SAYS

Simon was prepared. Mr. Nebble was handsome, suave, rich, smart, and something else. Simon thought that "something else" was up to no good. He couldn't be sure, but he was determined not to leave him and his sister in harm's way. The bad thing was that there was just no time to warn his sister. The engine was whining so loudly that she couldn't have heard him anyway.

And so that's how Mr. Nebble suddenly became trapped in his own airplane, when Simon tied a nice big nautical knot in one end of the tarp and attached it to the straps holding the pilot in his harness. The more he tugged, the tighter the pilot pulled himself into the trap.

"Sorry," Simon said, as he skirted the man's flailing arm. He shoved his shocked sister toward the door and tossed her out of the plane!

Frederica landed in a patch of sand. She was not hurt, but she was surprised and angry. "Simmmmmmmon!" she squealed.

"Run for the house!" her brother ordered. Then, he, too, plopped down in the sand, slamming the plane door behind him.

Fortunately the cockpit was facing away from the house. Mathilda came running. "Laws, laws, you kids, where have you been? Not in that plane? Where's Mr. Nebble?" She was in a dither.

Simon brushed himself off and tried to act in control. "Oh, I think he's heading on to New York. He's running late. He said for us to have our cocoa and cookies in the sunroom now."

Frederica looked astounded, but she followed her brother's lead. Mathilda, perturbed and confused, ignored the airplane. After all, her boss flew in and out of Oatfields at all times of the day and night. But children! Children on Oatfields. It was a first. She could hardly wait to feed them!

And the children could hardly wait to eat. So it was with bitter disappointment when Mathilda headed from the kitchen to the sunroom with a tray of sandwiches, cookies, lemonade, and hot chocolate...that Simon shoved his sister out of another side door, around the house, and told her to make a run for the dock.

"Simon," Frederica pleaded. But she knew that they had to flee and flee fast.

However, neither of them were prepared for what greeted them at the edge of the island where they had come ashore. Now, this boat had sunk!

CHAPTER EIGHTEEN

LAND'S END

Simon was angry now. He refused to be defeated. Slashing about in the water, he retrieved what was left of the boat. When they had a dozen good-sized boards and a handful of line, Simon spotted the knife in the cord grass and began to hack and cut and tie.

Quickly, Frederica realized what her brother was doing and helped him. Very soon, they had a raft. Well, it was a small square of wet boards with a rudder lashed to the back, and two board oars.

"We won't get far on this," Frederica said. "Not even Tom Sawyer and Huckleberry Finn could get far on this contraption."

"We don't have to get far," Simon said, climbing aboard and pulling his sister up behind him. "We just have to get away."

"And get to Eyesocket Island?" Frederica asked. For the first time, she was really afraid. Surely Mother Nature had not created an island that looked like a skull from the air. Surely it was man-made. That meant it was inhabited. And Frederica had a strong suspicion that if anyone was on that island, they were up to no good. No good at all.

It didn't matter. Just off the coast another storm was brewing, headed their way. The clouds grew dark and low and spit lightning. Hail pelted down upon the children. The thunder was deafening. The wind shoved the raft this way and that. One gust pushed up beneath the raft and all but pitch-poled them end over end.

It grew dark. Slowly, one by one, the slats that made up the raft came untied and floated away. Simon and Frederica held on to what little was left of the small pile of boards, until with one swash of a large wave, they were holding on only to one another.

CHAPTER NINETEEN

DAYBREAK

When daylight came, the two children could hardly move. The raft had completely disappeared or disintegrated. But they had been shoved by the big wave up onto a small hammock of dry land.

"I have sand in my underwear," Frederica grumbled. She hated, absolutely hated, sand in her underwear!

Simon moaned. "I have sand in my ears. In my eyes. In my nose."

Suddenly Frederica began to cry.

"Hey," Simon said, "I'm ok. You're ok. It's ok. We didn't drown. Please don't cry." He hated when girls cried.

His sister shook her head, slinging sand from her hair. "It's not ok!" she insisted. "The book's gone, isn't it? Dad's clues—gone. All our money gone. What will we do now?"

Simon looked around. It was true, the book had probably blown or floated away, page by page, into the storm. Dad couldn't help them now. No one could.

"Aw, c'mon," Simon pleaded, trying to sound braver than he felt. "We'll do that Robinson Crusoe thing. You know, like when the Swiss Family Robinson was marooned on an island. We'll build a shelter and catch fish and send out notes in a bottle."

Frederica stood up unsteadily. She shook herself like a wet puppy, dislodging sand in every direction. "Simon," she said, "you spend too much time in the library. This is not fiction. This is real life. You know, where we get dehydrated and starve and..."

Before she could finish her sentence, Frederica froze. Simon did as well. Quietly, they hunkered back down, trying to hide themselves in the marsh. They could hear something stalking toward them. It was a very deliberate sound. It was headed directly toward them.

Just then, the red blob of sun burst over the horizon. Silhouetted in front of it, a dark figure appeared. The stalking sound continued. Then the figure stopped right in front of them.

"Oh, no," said Simon, disgusted. "We can't get a break. Surely this is not what it seems?"

"Oh, yeah, Simon, it's what it seems," Frederica said. "It's just what you think it is. It's a dadgum pirate!"

"Avast, sandy maties!" a voice boomed at them.

CHAPTER TWENTY

AVAST AGAIN!

Simon had just about had it. "So, what?" he demanded, too tired and hungry and sandy to be afraid. "You gonna make us walk the plank, or something?"

The deep voice roared. The figure removed the enormous hat it wore. The big, black boots moved closer. Just then, the sun inched a little higher in the sky and the kids could actually see their nemesis.

"You?" said Simon.

"You're a pirate?" asked Frederica. She tried not to laugh.

The scrawny, old man looked **bashful**, like his feelings were hurt. His hat was just straw and his "boots" sandals with reed straps wound up skinny legs to bony knees. He was even more wrinkled than Miz Emmeline. And he was as tan as polished furniture.

"Yes, me," he whined. "Who'd you think? But Miz Emmeline said you wouldn't be coming out here. Said it would be dangerous. But I'd hoped you'd come to rescue Ben. I'm too old for all this."

Now Simon was alert and interested. "Too old for what, Ben? Ben, that's your name, isn't it?"

The man looked as if he could not remember. He seemed as addled as Miz Emmeline, maybe more so. He did not look well. "Ben, that's me," he finally agreed.

"Are we on Eyesocket Island, Ben?" asked Frederica.

"Aye," said Ben, "Eyesocket. I'm so tired of Eyesocket."

"What do you do here, Ben?" Simon asked softly. "Who do you do it for?"

Now the old man swung around rapidly. He looked totally petrified. "Not supposed to tell," he said. "Shhh. Not supposed to let anyone know."

Quickly, Frederica tried another tack. "Ben, how do you know Miz Emmeline? Do you help her?"

Ben grinned a snaggletooth smile. He seemed to swoon. "Ayyyye," he said. "I love Miz Emmeline. We were sweethearts, once."

The kids exchanged glances, but tried not to giggle. They couldn't imagine Ben and Miz Emmeline being sweethearts, but maybe that had been long ago when both were young. Maybe even at Chocolate Plantation.

"So you help her because you like her?" Frederica egged him on.

"Aye! Aye!" cried Ben merrily. "I'm not supposed to leave but every full moon, I take my skiff over to Miz Emmeline's tugboat and take her supplies and fresh water. And fish, if I catch any."

Simon stood up. "You have a skiff, Ben?"

Ben looked wary. "It's ok," he whimpered. "It's my skiff."

"Oh, that's ok, we understand," said Frederica. "Why don't you show it to us? And what kind of supplies do you have?"

Ben stood proud and slammed the straw hat back on his head and tightened the ratty, faded bandanna around his neck. "Why everything you want!" he said. "Food...and..."

But before he could continue, both kids jumped up and hugged the old man. "You have food, Ben? Food?" Simon pleaded.

Ben grinned again. "O'course I got food. Want some?"

CHAPTER
TWENTY ONE

EYESOCKET
ISLAND

Soon, they were following Ben through marshy passages that he seemed to know like the back of his hand. In fact, the old man sped so quickly across the island that the children could hardly keep up.

They thought they might see the clear pools of water that made up Eyesocket's eyes, or perhaps the skiff of sand nose. They did see wild horses scampering in the distance. But Ben took them directly to the craggy mouth.

It was not a mouth at all. It was an ugly scar gouged out of the marsh and sea oats. Shovels and picks were scattered around...work gloves...diagrams. The children were totally confused.

"Ben, what are you digging for?" Simon asked. "Buried treasure?"

For a long moment, Ben was quiet and thoughtful. "Sorta," he finally admitted. Frederica and Simon exchanged glances. Was this what Dad had hoped they would find—long lost buried pirate treasure?!

Then Ben shook his head, "No," he said. "Not pirate treasure. No pirates—just me. They told me to pretend I was a pirate if anyone ever saw me."

"Who told you that?" asked Frederica eagerly.

"The men," said Ben, matter-of-factly.

"What men?" Simon asked, afraid he already knew who one of them was.

Ben rubbed the stubble of beard that shadowed his chin. "The men in suits. They brought me here after I got in some trouble ashore. Brought me supplies. Come now and then. Scare me, but they need me."

"They need you?" Frederica asked, puzzled. "What do they need you for?" she asked. It was hard to imagine.

Ben got his proud look on his face again. "To find the bomb, o'course," he said.

Simon and Frederica looked around at the picks and shovels and disturbed dirt that surrounded them.

"The bomb?" said Frederica, hoarsely.

"The bomb?" repeated Simon. "What bomb, Ben? *What bomb?!*"

CHAPTER TWENTY TWO

BOMBS AWAY

The kids were jittery as Ben opened can after can of clam chowder. But it was delicious, even cold out of the can, and they shoveled spoonfuls of it into their mouths while Ben rattled on.

"I was in the military. Back when a plane crashed (he waved an arm seaward) and the bomb escaped," Ben explained. "No one could ever find it. No one wanted to say if it was really armed or not. World War II, you know. But they looked and looked and then gave up."

"So why did they want you to look some more now?" asked Simon, between bites.

"The radiation, o'course," said Ben. "Maybe the radiation was leaking."

At first Frederica was scared. Radiation? That couldn't be a good thing. Then she thought about it. "But, Ben, if there really was radiation, they could detect it I think, by now, with some sophisticated instruments. Are you sure that's why the men in the suits told you to look for the bomb?"

Ben looked nervous now and puzzled.

Simon said, "That's right, Fred.   But the radiation comes from a source and maybe that's what the men really have Ben looking for.   Plutonium or something they could sell for millions on the international terrorism market, or something."

Well, Frederica thought to herself, they could worry about a bomb or radiation or even plutonium, but she thought there was something that they should worry about a lot more. "Ben," she said, "how often do the men in suits come to see you?"

The old man slapped his thigh with his hand, proud he knew the answer to this question. "When there's no moon," he said.   "That's why I take Miz Emmeline her supplies on the full moon. Then I can be back when it's dark. They come then."

Simon had no doubt that this old salt knew the tides and the cycles of the moon like the back of his withered hands. He felt sure that Ben had been smart and strong in his day, only now he was old and had made some mistake, and been tricked into coming out here; heaven knows for how long. Like Miz Emmeline, old age and dementia kept him just enough in the dark that he did not question what was asked of him or realize how many years might have gone by while he toiled on Eyesocket Island.

"Eyesocket's not on the map, is it, Ben?" asked Simon.

"Nope!" said Ben, matter-of-factly. "As far as the military is concerned, this island doesn't exist. I guess you could say it just fell into the sea, or something." He laughed.

Frederica looked puzzled until her brother said, "Classified. The military could do that. I remember Dad talking about an airplane that flew off course off this coast and disappeared. It had a bomb aboard, but the military insisted that it was unarmed and not dangerous. Every now and then there's an article about it in the newspaper, but it was never found."

Ben surprised them by looking angry, very angry. It scared them. "Was too found!" he shouted. "Was, too. Should know. I found it!"

And to their surprise, Ben scraped away a little of the sandy earth beside them, and an old piece of metal—clearly part of a larger object—appeared.

Frederica thought she would faint! But before she did, she asked Ben one last question. "Ben, when is it dark again?"

The old man had faded back into his abstract, distracted world. But still, he answered with certainty. "Tonight," he said. "Tonight's dark."

CHAPTER TWENTY THREE

DARK OF THE MOON

It was strange how it all ended up. Ben was right, it was the dark of the moon that night. But for the rest of the day, the old man and the kids were exceedingly busy. It took awhile, but the trap was set. And when Mr. Nebble and his friends showed up that night, well, they got the surprise of their life!

Ben knew exactly where they came ashore in their small, sleek boat with a high-powered, but quiet motor. He said they did the same thing every time—tied up, stalked ashore, and came directly to the "dig," as he called it. They made Ben show them what he had, or had not, found. They had not yet seen the bomb, because Ben had never told them he'd found it! He always just showed them the latest empty hole he was digging.

But this time, Ben showed them the piece of exposed bomb. The men were so excited that they never noticed Ben move out of the way, nor the children and Ben pull the lines that trapped them all into an elaborate net. They cursed mightily, especially Mr. Nebble. In fact, he squirmed and screamed so much that a cell phone fell from his pocket.

When Simon spied it, he scrambled beneath the net, careful to keep just out of reach, and grabbed it. He and his sister knew whom to call, and it was no time at all before Pedro, the U.S. Coast Guard helicopter, was landing nearby.

"Dad didn't really send us on a vision quest, did he?" Frederica asked her brother, as the men were handcuffed and hauled aboard the helicopter.

"What do you mean?" asked Simon.

Frederica nodded at Ben, who looked very tired, but was smiling. "I mean I think he sent us on a rescue mission."

"Yeah," said Simon, "maybe. But who's gonna rescue *us*?"

In a moment, that question was answered when another Coast Guard helicopter appeared. It landed nearby and cut its engine. Slowly, the blades whispered to a stop. The door opened and a man dressed in fishing gear stepped out.

"Dad?" cried Frederica. "Dad!"

"I heard the distress call," he said. "Cap'n Rogers' boat was just offshore. He called the Coast Guard for me. Let's go home!"

POSTLOGUE

Let's see:

Ben and Miz Emmeline got married—aboard the *Lady Bee*, then moved to a nice nursing home in Savannah.

Mathilda knew a lot more than the average housekeeper and "told all" at the trial—with lots of "laws, laws," thrown in for good measure! Mr. Nebble and his friends went to prison.

Simon grew up and went to law school. He hasn't decided what area he'd like to specialize in yet. He might also become a pilot, he says.

Frederica became a famous local artist. Her pottery is exhibited in some of the nicer galleries on the coast. She gave the first piece she ever "threw" to Ben and Miz Emmeline as a wedding present. They keep chocolate chip cookies in it.

Dan Brickhill admitted he never meant for their adventure to get so risky or so far from home. He apologized quite a lot in his later years, as if the remembrance caused him grief, but his children assured him that they would not have traded their "vision quest" adventure for anything.

Oatfields was turned into an Atlantic Right Whale research laboratory and wild horse sanctuary.

And the bomb?

What bomb?

about the author

Carole Marsh is an author and publisher who has written many works of fiction and non-fiction for young readers. She travels throughout the United States and around the world to research her books. In 1979 Carole Marsh was named Communicator of the Year for her corporate communications work with major national and international corporations.

Marsh is the founder and CEO of Gallopade International, established in 1979. Today, Gallopade International is widely recognized as a leading source of educational materials for every state and many countries. Marsh and Gallopade were recipients of the 2004 Teachers' Choice Award. Marsh has written more than 50 Carole Marsh Mysteries™. In 2007, she was named Georgia Author of the Year. Years ago, her children, Michele and Michael, were the original characters in her mystery books. Today, they continue the Carole Marsh Books tradition by working at Gallopade. By adding grandchildren Grant and Christina as new mystery characters, she has continued the tradition for a third generation.

Ms. Marsh welcomes correspondence from her readers. You can e-mail her at fanclub@gallopade.com, visit carolemarshmysteries.com, or write to her in care of Gallopade International, P.O. Box 2779, Peachtree City, Georgia, 30269 USA.

built-in book Club
talk about it!

Questions for Discussion

1. Simon and Frederica live in a cabin in an isolated fishing village. They are alone a lot because their father is out fishing. Would you like to live a life like that? Why or why not?

2. How did you feel when the children's father left them? How would you have felt if it happened to you?

3. Did you think it was a good idea or a bad idea for Simon to buy the first boat and spend half of the money their father had given them? Why did you think that?

4. Why would an alligator be especially dangerous if it was guarding a nest?

5. Why does someone like Miz Emmeline live on an old ship? Why doesn't she live in a house?

6. Why did the kids hide on Mr. Nebble's airplane? How did that end up helping them on their vision quest?

7. If you wrote your own "Pretty Darn Scary" mystery, what real place would you choose for the setting?

8. Which parts of this story do you think the author made up? Which parts do you think are true?

built-in book Club
bring it to life!

Activities to Do

1. Did you enjoy the stories in the Postlogue about what happened to the characters later in life? Write your own Postlogue! Make up new stories about what happened to Ben, Miz Emmeline, Mathilda, Mr. Nebble, Simon, Frederica, and their dad.

2. Draw a picture of Simon and Frederica riding in the boat they bought when they first started on their journey. Remember it was described as a "piece of junk" with "rusted spots near the bow."

3. Remember how the children loved the warm chocolate chip cookies that Miz Emmeline served

them? Make some chocolate chip cookies of your own to share in your next Book Club meeting. You can find a recipe online, or you can probably find one on the back of a package of chocolate chips.

4. Create your own Eyesocket Island! Mold modeling clay into the perfect shape, and cut out the eyes, nose and mouth. Then, paint your island in your choice of colors!

5. Write a journal page for Dan Brickhill, the father of Simon and Frederica. Describe a day in the life of a fisherman. Include how it feels to get up before dawn, set out in a boat in the stillness of the morning, spend hours in the blinding sun without catching one fish, and the excitement of catching one really big fish before heading home for the night!

6. Do some research on Spanish moss. It's pretty cool stuff! What is it, exactly? Where does it grow? How does it live? Do bugs live in it? Will it survive inside your house?

Pretty darn Scary

glossary

 abhor: to dislike intensely

 bashful: timid or shy

 compliment: something said when a person wants to praise or admire

desolate: not lived in or deserted; or very unhappy

dry-dock: to remove a ship from water so that work can be done on it

emaciated: very thin, especially from disease, hunger, or cold

feral: describes a domestic animal that has returned to a wild state

gunkhole: to explore creeks, coves, or marshes near the shore

sieve: a strainer used to separate liquids from solids or tiny pieces from large ones

wetlands: tidal areas or swamps that tend to be regularly wet or flooded

tech
Connects

Useful Websites to Visit

On the Georgia coastal barrier islands...
http://crd.dnr.state.ga.us/content/displaycontent.asp?
txtDocument=422
http://www.georgiaencyclopedia.org/nge/Article.jsp?
id=h-2123

On Chocolate Plantation...
http://www.yahoolavista.com/sapeloisland/tabby-
ruins/index.html

More Resources
The Georgia Coast: Waterways and Islands
by Nancy Schwalbe Zydler and Tom Zydler

A Guide to a Georgia Barrier Island
by Taylor Schoettle

Visit carolemarshmysteries.com
for fun reproducible activities!

enjoy this excerpt from...

The Ghosts of
Pickpocket
Plantation

by Carole Marsh

CHAPTER ONE

his name was telesphore

HIS NAME WAS TELESPHORE. He had no idea why his grandmother had named him that. His grandmother had to name him because his mother had died giving birth to him. His father was nowhere to be found. No name had been selected, not even hinted at, much less batted about from some charming book of baby names. So his grandmother named him Telesphore. Thank goodness his friends called him Terry. But somehow, deep underneath, he felt like Telesphore, a name that seemed auspicious, but also a burden. But he couldn't think of that now. Now he had to think of snakes.

Water moccasins were part and parcel of the peat bog swamp that surrounded Pickpocket Plantation. So were alligators. Mosquitoes the size of saucers. Wild turkeys. And, rarely, a wild boar.

"Watch where you s.....t......e......p," Terry reminded himself. His Aunt Penelope had lent him a beat-up old pair of hightop, lace-up boots, but he figured a diamondback rattler's fangs could easily pierce right through the leather as if it were butter. Terry realized that he had involuntarily squiggled his feet so far back up into his shoes that his toes were cramping. "Step carefully," he whispered to himself.

Terry wondered how anyone had ever gotten anything done going tippy-toe around the enormous plantation acreage. "Shoot," he said aloud, again to himself, "I will just stomp along like brave Huck Finn might have done and take what comes." As he walked more willfully, he tried to recall if Tom Sawyer and Huck Finn had been more brave, or cowardly. Either way, they were on the Mississippi River, and Terry did not think alligators the length of small cars had ever worried them, except perhaps in their imaginations.

In Terry's imagination, he was scouting out Pickpocket as it must have been in the days of the Yamacraw Indians, or in the painful era of plantation slavery, or during the wily time of the Civil War (the War of Northern Aggression, as some old-time southerners still called it), or some other time of historic excitement. But, really, Terry knew in his heart that he was just trying not to be bored.

Or scared. After all, didn't Aunt Penelope say that the Saturday *Savannah Pilot* recently featured a story about a fisherman poling his skiff through some snarled morass of wetland weeds getting his foot chomped off by a gator?

"Step carefully, Terry...

c   a   r   e   f   u   l   l   y."

enjoy this excerpt from...

THE MYSTERY AT FORT THUNDERBOLT

by Carole Marsh

#3

CHAPTER THREE

THUNDERBOLT: TIM

"Hey, you gonna get Big Red and get my boat in?" A burly, sunburned man of about sixty asked the question in a demanding Yankee accent.

"You're next," Tim said flatly. He was respectful to those at the Thunderbolt Marina who were nice to him and his sister, who both worked there after school. He was never disrespectful to the rude ones, but he offered no apologies. They had to wait their turn like everyone else.

Thunderbolt Marina was in the town of Thunderbolt, an old fishing community on the ICW (the Intracoastal Waterway) which wound all along this part of the coast. A dashed line on nautical charts marked the ICW, a channel of water boats could use to travel inland along the coast instead of going "outside," meaning in the Atlantic Ocean.

Any marina on the ICW was always busy, especially in spring or fall. In the fall, many boats traveled from colder states in the northeast down to warmer climes in Florida, or even on to the Bahamas. In the spring, the parade reversed itself and the boats scampered back to their home waters for the summer season.

All Tim knew was that lots of folks had boats, but not everyone actually knew how to boat. On the ICW you had everything from the big shrimp trawlers and long, skinny barges, to multi-million dollar motor yachts crewed by teams in matching polo shirts, to sailboats tall and small, to runabouts pulling skiers, and jet skiers buzzing around them all like bumblebees. It looked like fun, but it was always a chance for disaster, as well.

"Thank you," the courteous owner of the *My Girl* said, tipping Tim with a twenty-dollar bill.

"Thank you, sir," Tim responded politely. He had just used Big Red, the marina forklift, to hoist the forty-footer into the launch area. "Let me know if you need any help getting your gear aboard, sir."

The man nodded his thanks and moved on. Tim ducked his head so the surly Yankee who was frowning big-time would not see the slight grin he just couldn't help. Tim knew from the marine radio monitoring the water traffic that the guy had run his big, new powerboat aground on one of the shifting sandbars in the sound and had been too impatient to wait for the high tide to float it off. His impatience had cost him an expensive tow into the marina the day before.

Today, he was here getting his boat back out of the boat barn so some even more expensive repair work could be done. Tim marveled at how some boaters (with more money than sense, to his way of thinking) got GPS (Global Positioning System) and other electronic gear loaded on their boat, but failed to learn to use it before they actually set out on the water.

If they had asked, Tim could tell them the truth: the water was unforgiving of ignorance. Just ask Sea Tow, who hauled in stranded or disabled boats all the time. Or Coast Guard Station Tybee, nearby, which sent the orange helicopter called *Pedro*, as well as boats and men, to the rescue. Or, he thought, no sign of a grin on his face now, ask him and Telly, who had lost their younger brother a few years back in a stupid boat accident in the Savannah River within sight of land.

There was no place for stupid on the water.

"Your boat's ready, sir," Tim said to the Yankee man, who swigged back another beer and stomped toward the gangway to the dock, never bothering to acknowledge the courtesy.

WRITE YOUR OWN MYSTERY!

Make up a dramatic title!

You can pick four real kid characters!

Select a real place for the story's setting!

Try writing your first draft!

Edit your first draft!

Read your final draft aloud!

You can add art, photos or illustrations!

Share your book with others and send me a copy!

WOULD YOU   LIKE TO BE
A CHARACTER IN A CAROLE MARSH MYSTERY?

If you would like to star in a Carole Marsh Mystery, fill out the form below and write a 25-word paragraph about why you think you would make a good character! Once you're done, ask your mom or dad to send this page to:

> Carole Marsh Mysteries Fan Club
> Gallopade International
> P.O. Box 2779
> Peachtree City, GA 30269

My name is: _____

I am a: _____boy _____ girl Age: _____

I live at: _____

City: _____ State:_____ Zip code: _____

My e-mail address: _____

My phone number is: _____

_____
_____
_____
_____
_____
_____
_____
_____
_____
_____

VISIT THE CAROLE MARSH MYSTERIES WEBSITE

www.carolemarshmysteries.com

- *Download these neat-o activity sheets:*
  - > Weave Your Very Own Web Page!
  - > What's Your Story?
  - > Make a Whale Mobile
  - > Bad Dude Blackbeard
  - > Coastal Island Crossword
- *Check out what's coming up next! Are we coming to your area with our next book release? Maybe you can have your book signed by the author!*
- *Join the Carole Marsh Mysteries Fan Club!*
- *Apply for the chance to be a character in an upcoming Carole Marsh Mystery!*
- *Learn how to write your own mystery!*